Born in Kasauli in 1934, Ruskin Bond grew up in Jamnagar, Dehradun, New Delhi and Shimla. His first novel, *The Room on the Roof*, written when he was seventeen, received the John Llewellyn Rhys Memorial Prize in 1957. Since then he has written over five hundred short stories, essays and novellas (some included in the collections *Dust on the Mountain* and *Classic Ruskin Bond*) and more than forty books for children.

He received the Sahitya Akademi Award for English writing in India in 1993, the Padma Shri in 1999 and the Delhi government's Lifetime Achievement Award in 2012. He was awarded the Sahitya Akademi's Bal Sahitya Puraskar for his 'total contribution to children's literature' in 2013 and was honoured with the Padma Bhushan in 2014. He lives in Landour, Mussoorie, with his extended family.

ALSO IN PUFFIN BY RUSKIN BOND

Getting Granny's Glasses

Earthquake

The Cherry Tree

The Eyes of the Eagle

Dust on the Mountain

Cricket for the Crocodile

Puffin Classics: The Room on the Roof

Puffin Classics: Vagrants in the Valley

The Room of Many Colours: A Treasury of Stories for Children

Panther's Moon and Other Stories

The Hidden Pool

The Parrot Who Wouldn't Talk and Other Stories

Mr Oliver's Diary

Escape from Java and Other Tales of Danger

Crazy Times with Uncle Ken

Rusty: The Boy from the Hills

Rusty Runs Away

Rusty and the Leopard

Rusty Goes to London

Rusty Comes Home

Rusty and the Magic Mountain

The Puffin Book of Classic School Stories

The Puffin Good Reading Guide for Children

The Kashmiri Storyteller

Hip-Hop Nature Boy and Other Poems

The Adventures of Rusty: Collected Stories

Thick as Thieves: Tales of Friendship

Uncles, Aunts and Elephants: Tales from Your Favourite Storyteller

Ranji's Wonderful Bat and Other Stories

Whispers in the Dark: A Book of Spooks

The Day Grandfather Tickled a Tiger

RUSKIN BOND

THE TREE LOVER

Illustrations by
Ahlawat Gunjan

PUFFIN BOOKS
An imprint of Penguin Random House

PUFFIN BOOKS

USA | Canada | UK | Ireland | Australia
New Zealand | India | South Africa | China

Penguin Books is part of the Penguin Random House group of companies
whose addresses can be found at global.penguinrandomhouse.com

Published by Penguin Random House India Pvt. Ltd
7th Floor, Infinity Tower C, DLF Cyber City,
Gurgaon 122 002, Haryana, India

Penguin
Random House
India

First published in Puffin Books as part of *The Room of Many Colours* by
Penguin Books India 2001
This illustrated edition published 2017

Text copyright © Ruskin Bond 2001
Illustrations copyright © Ahlawat Gunjan 2017

ISBN 9780143428749

Typeset in Adobe Garamond Pro
Book design by Ahlawat Gunjan
Printed at Aarvee Promotions India

www.penguin.co.in

CHAPTER 1

I was never able to get over the feeling that plants and trees loved Grandfather with as much tenderness as he loved them. I was sitting beside him on the veranda steps one morning, when I noticed the tendril of a creeping vine that was trailing near my feet. As we sat there, in the soft sunshine of a north Indian winter, I saw that the tendril was moving very slowly away from me and towards Grandfather. Twenty minutes later it had crossed the veranda step and was touching Grandfather's feet.

There is probably a scientific explanation for the plant's behaviour—something to do with light and warmth—but I like to think that it moved that way simply because it was fond of Grandfather. One felt like drawing close to him. Sometimes when I sat alone beneath a tree I would feel a little lonely or lost; but as soon as Grandfather joined me, the garden would become a happy place, the tree itself more friendly.

CHAPTER 2

Grandfather had served many years in the Indian Forest Service, and so it was natural that he should know and understand and like trees. On his retirement from the Service, he had built a bungalow on the outskirts of Dehra, planting trees all round it: limes, mangoes, oranges and guavas; also eucalyptus, jacaranda and the Persian lilac. In the fertile Doon valley, plants and trees grew tall and strong. There were other trees in the compound before the house was built, including an old peepul

which had forced its way through the walls of an abandoned outhouse, knocking the bricks down with its vigorous growth. Peepul trees are great show-offs. Even when there is no breeze, their broadchested, slim-waisted leaves will spin like tops, determined to attract your attention and invite you into the shade.

Grandmother had wanted the peepul tree cut down, but Grandfather had said, 'Let it be. We can always build another outhouse.'

The gardener, Dukhi, who was a Hindu, was pleased that we had allowed the tree to live. Peepul trees are sacred to Hindus, and some people believe that ghosts live in the branches. 'If we cut the tree down, wouldn't the ghosts go away?' I asked.

'I don't know,' said Grandfather. 'Perhaps they'd come into the house.'

Dukhi wouldn't walk under the tree at night. He said that once, when he was young, he had wandered beneath a peepul tree late at night, and that something heavy had fallen with a thud on his shoulders. Since then he had always walked with a slight stoop, he explained.

'Nonsense,' said Grandmother, who didn't believe in ghosts. 'He got his stoop from squatting on his haunches year after year, weeding with that tiny spade of his!'

I never saw any ghosts in our peepul tree. There are peepul trees all over India, and people sometimes leave offerings of milk and flowers beneath them to keep the spirits happy. But since no one left any offerings under our tree, I expect the ghosts left in disgust, to look for peepul trees where there was both board and lodging.

Grandfather was about sixty, a lean active man who still rode his bicycle at great speed. He had stopped climbing trees only a year ago when he had got to the top of the jackfruit tree and had been unable to come down again. We had to fetch a ladder for him.

Grandfather bathed quite often but got back into his gardening clothes immediately after the bath. During meals, ladybirds or caterpillars would sometimes walk off his shirtsleeves and wander about on the tablecloth, and this always annoyed Grandmother.

She grumbled at Grandfather a lot, but he didn't mind, because he knew she loved him.

My favourite tree was the banyan which grew behind the house. Its spreading branches, which hung to the ground and took root again, formed a number of twisting passageways. The tree was older than the house, older than my grandparents; I could hide in its branches, behind a screen of thick green leaves, and spy on the world below.

The banyan tree was a world in itself, populated with small animals and large insects. While the leaves were still pink and tender, they would be visited by the delicate map butterfly, who left her eggs in their care. The 'honey' on the leaves—a sweet, sticky smear—also attracted the little striped squirrels, who soon grew used to having me in the tree and became quite bold, accepting gram from my hand.

At night the tree was visited by the hawk cuckoo. Its shrill, nagging cry kept us awake on hot summer nights. Indians called the bird 'Paos-ala', which means 'Rain is coming!' But according to Grandfather, when the bird was in full cry, it seemed to be shouting, 'Oh dear, oh dear! How very hot it's getting! We feel it . . . we feel it . . . WE FEEL IT!'

CHAPTER 3

Grandfather wasn't content with planting trees in our garden. During the rains we would walk into the jungle beyond the riverbed, armed with cuttings and saplings, and these we would plant in the forest, beside the tall sal and shisham trees.

'But no one ever comes here,' I protested, the first time we did this. 'Who is going to see them?'

'We're not planting for people only,' said Grandfather. 'We're planting for the forest—

and for the birds and animals who live here and need more food and shelter.'

He told me how men, and not only birds and animals, needed trees—for keeping the desert away, for attracting rain, for preventing the banks of rivers from being washed away, and for wild plants and grasses to grow beneath.

'And for timber?' I asked, pointing to the sal and shisham trees.

'Yes, and for timber. But men are cutting down the trees without replacing them. For every tree that's felled, we must plant two. Otherwise, one day there'll be no forests at all, and the world will become one great desert.'

The thought of a world without trees became a sort of nightmare for me—it's one reason why I shall never want to live on the treeless Moon—and I helped Grandfather in his tree planting with even greater enthusiasm. He taught me a poem by George Morris, and we would recite it together:

WOODMAN, SPARE THAT TREE!
TOUCH NOT A SINGLE BOUGH!
IN YOUTH IT SHELTERED ME,
AND I'LL PROTECT IT NOW.

'One day the trees will move again,' said Grandfather. 'They've been standing still for thousands of years, but one day they'll move again. There was a time when trees could walk about like people, but along came the Devil and cast a spell over them, rooting them to one place. But they're always trying to move—see how they reach out with their arms—and some of them, like the banyan tree with its travelling roots, manage to get quite far!'

In the autumn, Grandfather took me to the hills. The deodars (Indian cedars), oaks, chestnuts and maples were very different from the trees I had grown up with in Dehra. The broad leaves of the horse chestnut had turned yellow, and smooth brown chestnuts lay scattered on the roads. Grandfather and

I filled our pockets with them, then climbed the slope of a bare hill and started planting the chestnuts in the ground.

I don't know if they ever came up, because I never went there again. Goats and cattle grazed freely on the hill, and, if the trees did come up

in the spring, they may well have been eaten; but I like to think that somewhere in the foothills of the Himalayas there is a grove of chestnut trees, and that birds and flying foxes and cicadas have made their homes in them.

CHAPTER 4

Back in Dehra, we found an island, a small rocky island in the middle of a dry riverbed. It was one of those riverbeds, so common in the Doon valley, which are completely dry in summer but flooded during the monsoon rains. A small mango tree was growing in the middle of the island, and Grandfather said, 'If a mango can grow here, so can other trees.'

As soon as the rains set in—and while the river could still be crossed—we set out with

a number of tamarind, laburnum and coral tree saplings and cuttings, and spent the day planting them on the island.

When the monsoon set in, the trees appeared to be flourishing.

The monsoon season was the time for rambling about. At every turn there was something new to see. Out of earth and rock and leafless bough, the magic touch of the monsoon rains had brought life and greenness.

You could almost see the broad-leaved vines grow. Plants sprang up in the most unlikely places. A peepul would take root in the ceiling, a mango would sprout on the windowsill. We did not like to remove them; but they had to go, if the house was to be kept from falling down.

'If you want to live in a tree, it's all right by me,' said Grandmother. 'But I like having a roof over my head, and I'm not going to have it brought down by the jungle!'

The common monsoon sights along the Indian roads were always picturesque—the wide plains, with great herds of smoke-coloured, delicate-limbed cattle being driven slowly home for the night, accompanied by several ungainly buffaloes, and flocks of goats and black long-tailed sheep.

Then you came to a pond, where some buffaloes were enjoying themselves, with no part of them visible but the tips of their noses, while on their backs were a number of merry children, perfectly and happily naked. The banyan tree really came to life during the monsoon, when the branches were thick with

scarlet figs. Humans couldn't eat the berries, but the many birds that gathered in the tree—gossipy rosy pastors, quarrelsome mynahs, cheerful bulbuls and coppersmiths, and sometimes a noisy, bullying crow—feasted on them. And when night fell and the birds were resting, the dark flying foxes flapped heavily about the tree, chewing and munching loudly as they clambered over the branches.

The tree crickets were a band of willing artists who started their singing at almost any time of the day but preferably in the evenings. Delicate pale green creatures with transparent wings, they were hard to find amongst the lush monsoon foliage; but once found, a tap on the bush or leaf on which one of them sat would put an immediate end to its performance.

At the height of the monsoon, the banyan tree was like an orchestra with the musicians constantly tuning up. Birds, insects and

squirrels welcomed the end of the hot weather and the cool quenching relief of the monsoon.

A toy flute in my hands, I would try adding my shrill piping to theirs. But they must have thought poorly of my piping, for, whenever I played, the birds and the insects kept a pained and puzzled silence.

CHAPTER 5

I wonder if they missed me when I went away—for when the War came, followed by the Independence of India, I was sent to a boarding school in the hills. Grandfather's house was put up for sale. During the holidays I went to live with my parents in Delhi, and it was from them I learnt that my grandparents had gone to England.

When I finished school, I too went to England with my parents, and was away from India for several years. But recently I was in Dehra again, and after first visiting the old house—where I found that the banyan tree had grown over the wall and along part of the pavement, almost as though it had tried to follow Grandfather—I walked out of town towards the riverbed.

It was February, and as I looked across the dry watercourse, my eye was caught by the spectacular red plumes of the coral blossom. In contrast to the dry riverbed, the island was a small green paradise. When I walked across to

the trees, I noticed that a number of squirrels had come to live in them. And a koel (a sort of crow-pheasant) challenged me with a mellow 'who-are-you, who-are you . . .'

But the trees seemed to know me. They whispered among themselves and beckoned me nearer. And looking around, I noticed that other small trees and wild plants and grasses had sprung up under the protection of the trees we had placed there.

The trees had multiplied! They were *walking*. In one small corner of the world, Grandfather's dream was coming true, and the trees were moving again.

MORE IN THE SERIES
BY RUSKIN BOND

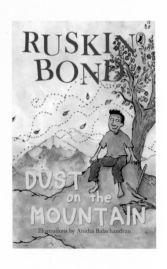

Bisnu finds how dangerous and lonely life can be for a boy who has to leave his home to earn money for his family. As he sets to work on the limestone quarries with the choking dust enveloping the beautiful mountain air, he longs for home more than ever.

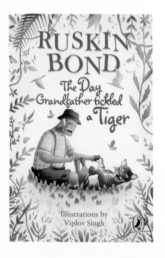

When Grandfather discovers a little tiger cub on a hunting expedition, he decides to take it home. Christened Timothy, the cub grows up as any regular house pet, with a monkey and a mongrel for company. But as he grows older, Timothy starts behaving strangely, and Grandfather decides that it's time to send him away.